SandCastle

Do Something About It!

Do Something in Your Country

Amanda Rondeau

Consulting Editor, Diane Craig, M.A./Reading Specialist

ABDO Publishing Company

Published by ABDO Publishing Company, 4940 Viking Drive, Edina, Minnesota 55435.

Printed in the United States.

Credits
Edited by: Pam Price
Curriculum Coordinator: Nancy Tuminelly
Cover and Interior Design and Production: Mighty Media
Photo Credits: BananaStock Ltd.,Corbis Images, Comstock, Digital Vision, PhotoDisc, Rubberball Productions, Skjold Photography

Library of Congress Cataloging-in-Publication Data

Rondeau, Amanda, 1974-.
Do something in your country / Amanda Rondeau.
p. cm.--(Do something about it!)
Includes index.
ISBN 1-59197-573-5
1. Child volunteers--Juvenile literature. 2. Social action--Juvenile literature. 3. Community development--Juvenile literature. 4. Quality of life--Juvenile literature. I. Title. II. Series.

HQ784.V64 R663 2004
361--dc21

2003058394

SandCastle™ books are created by a professional team of educators, reading specialists, and content developers around five essential components that include phonemic awareness, phonics, vocabulary, text comprehension, and fluency. All books are written, reviewed, and leveled for guided reading, early intervention reading, and Accelerated Reader® programs and designed for use in shared, guided, and independent reading and writing activities to support a balanced approach to literacy instruction.

Let Us Know

After reading the book, SandCastle would like you to tell us your stories about reading. What is your favorite page? Was there something hard that you needed help with? Share the ups and downs of learning to read. We want to hear from you! To get posted on the ABDO Publishing Company Web site, send us e-mail at:

sandcastle@abdopub.com

SandCastle Level: Transitional

You can make a difference in your country by doing something to make it a better place to live.

When you do something to help others, you are making a difference.

Mr. Draper wants the government to make more national parks.

He writes letters to his senators asking them to vote for more parks.

MARWICK
THE
sixties
OXFORD
Richard Dawkins
Un weaving the Rain bow
FAGAN
FLOODS, FAMINES AND EMPERORS
THE WAY OF THE WORLD
DAVID FROMKIN
KNOPF
BLIND MAN'S BLUFF
THE MONK AND THE PHILOSOPHER
A FATHER AND SON DISCUSS THE MEANING OF LIFE
The GOOD MAN of NANKING
THE DIARIES OF JOHN RABE
Earth Odyssey
Hertsgaard
PAULA GUNN ALLEN
off the
RESERVATION

Ms. Hoffman wants everyone to have books to read.

She collects donated books and sends them to libraries in other states.

Mr. Beck and Ms. Unger want to help protect homes from a flood.

They fill sandbags to hold the water back.

Mr. Michaels wants to protect wildlife from pollution.

He tells senators about the dangers of pollution.

Hailey is worried about plans to build a parking lot on a local marsh.

She writes a letter to her state representatives to tell them what she thinks.

Jane, Sue, and Ann want to protect whales.

They started a petition and will send it to the president.

Brett cares about people who don't have enough food.

He delivers food to people who are hungry.

Art Kit

Lily read about kids whose homes were damaged by a storm.

She and her friends make art kits so those kids will have something fun to do.

There are many ways you can make a difference in your country.

What would you like to do?

Glossary

country. a nation with its own government

donate. to give a gift to charity

flood. the rising and overflowing of a body of water such as a river or lake

government. the group of people who make the laws and policies that rule a city, state, or country

marsh. a low area of soft, wet land

petition. a written request signed by many people, often to try to change a policy or tell others how they feel about something

pollution. the act of contaminating air, water, or soil with man-made waste

president. the person elected to lead a country, company, or organization

representative. in government, a person we elect to speak for us, in the state or national house of representatives

sandbag. a bag filled with sand and used a protection, often against floodwaters

senator. in government, a person elected to the senate, a group of people that makes laws at the state or national level

About SandCastle™

A professional team of educators, reading specialists, and content developers created the SandCastle™ series to support young readers as they develop reading skills and strategies and increase their general knowledge. The SandCastle™ series has four levels that correspond to early literacy development in young children. The levels are provided to help teachers and parents select the appropriate books for young readers.

Emerging Readers
(no flags)

Beginning Readers
(1 flag)

Transitional Readers
(2 flags)

Fluent Readers
(3 flags)

These levels are meant only as a guide. All levels are subject to change.

ABDO Publishing Company

To see a complete list of SandCastle™ books and other nonfiction titles from ABDO Publishing Company, visit www.abdopub.com or contact us at:

4940 Viking Drive, Edina, Minnesota 55435 • 1-800-800-1312 • fax: 1-952-831-1632